MODELL

Knots on a Counting Rope

By Bill Martin Jr. and John Archambault

Illustrated by Ted Rand

SCHOLASTIC INC.
New York Toronto London Auckland Sydney
Mexico City New Delhi Hong Kong

Tell me the story again, Grandfather.
Tell me who I am.

> I have told you many times, Boy.
> You know the story by heart.

But it sounds better
when you tell it, Grandfather.

> Then listen carefully.
> This may be the last telling.

No, no, Grandfather.
There will never be a last time
Promise me that.
Promise me.

> I promise you nothing, Boy.
> I love you.
> That is better than a promise.

And I love you, Grandfather,
but tell me the story again.
Please.

Once there was a boy child . . .

No, Grandfather.
Start at the beginning.
Start where the storm
was crying my name.

You know the story, Boy.
Tell it.

No, Grandfather, no.
Start, "It was a dark night . . ."

It was a dark night,
a strange night.
Your mother and father and I
were safe in the hogan . . .

. . . and the sheep were safe
in the pen . . .

. . . when a wild storm
came out of the mountains . . .

. . . crying,
"Boy-eeeeeeeee! Boy-eeeeeeeee!"

. . . and your mother said,
"I hear it in the wounded wind.
A boy child will be born tonight."

Then what happened, Grandfather?

> I rode up the canyon fast,
> to bring the grandmother.
> It is not a good sign
> for a child to be born
> without a grandmother's blessing.

Was the wind still calling for me,
Grandfather?

> Yes, Boy, it was whipping up sand
> as sharp as claws,
> and crying like a bobcat,
> "Boy-eeeeeeeee! Boy-eeeeeeeee!"

Were you afraid, Grandfather?

> I was much afraid.

How much afraid?

> Heart-pounding afraid, Boy.

Then what happened, Grandfather?
Just as I was born . . .
tell me that part.

      It was strange . . . strange.
      Just as you came forth
      and made your first cry,
      the wind stopped howling
      and the storm was over . . .

. . . and the night became as quiet
as soft falling snow . . .

      . . . The grandmother took you up
      in her arms, and said,
      "He will walk in beauty . . .
      to the east . . ."

". . . to the west,
to the north, to the south,
he will walk in beauty . . ."

      ". . . forever."

And I was born strong,
wasn't I, Grandfather?

      No, you were not strong.
      You were sick and frail.
      We thought you would die.

But I didn't die, did I?
Tell me about that, Grandfather.

All night you lay silent
with your eyes closed,
your breath too shallow,
too weak for crying . . .

. . . and you carried me out
to see the morning, Grandfather,
but I did not open my eyes.
Tell me that part.

Two great blue horses
came galloping by . . .

. . . and they stopped, Grandfather!
They stopped and looked at me . . .

. . . and you raised your arms
to the great blue horses,
and I said,
"See how the horses speak to him.
They are his brothers from . . ."

". . . from beyond the dark mountains.
This boy child will not die."
That is what you said,
isn't it, Grandfather?

Yes, Boy, that is what I said,
"This boy child will not die.
The great blue horses have given him
the strength to live."

And that is when you named me,
isn't it, Grandfather?

> After you smiled your first smile,
> we had the naming ceremony.
> All of the grandmothers
> and grandfathers were there.

And you named me
Boy-Strength-of-Blue-Horses.

> It is a strong name.

Did I need a strong name,
Grandfather?

> All children need a strong name
> to help them grow strong.

And I grew strong, didn't I?

> Yes, Boy-Strength-of-Blue-Horses,
> and each day
> you are growing stronger.
> You are learning to cross
> the dark mountains.

I already have crossed
some of the dark mountains.

> There will be more, Boy.
> Dark mountains
> are always around us.
> They have no beginnings and . . .

. . . they have no endings.
But we know they are there, Grandfather,
when we suddenly feel afraid.

> Yes, Boy . . . afraid to do
> what we have to do.

Will I always have to live in the dark?

> Yes, Boy.
> You were born with a dark curtain
> in front of your eyes.

But there are many ways to see,
Grandfather.

> Yes, Boy, you are learning
> to see through your darkness
> because you have
> the strength of blue horses.

I see the horses with my hands,
Grandfather,
but I cannot see the blue.
What is *blue?*

  You know *morning*, Boy.

Yes, I can feel *morning*.
Morning throws off
the blanket of night.

  And you know *sunrise*.

Yes, I hear *sunrise*,
in the song of the birds.

  And you know *sky*, Boy.

Yes, *sky* touches my face . . .
soft, like lambs' wool . . .
and I breathe its softness.

  Blue is all of these.
  Blue is the feeling
  of a spring day beginning.
  Try . . . try to see it, Boy.

Blue? . . . blue?
Blue is the morning . . .
the sunrise . . .
the sky . . .
the song of the birds . . .
O, I see it!
Blue! Blue!
Blue is happiness, Grandfather!
I feel it . . . .
in my heart!

There was a sweep of blue
in the rainbow, Boy,
that morning your horse was born.

O, tell me that part, Grandfather!
I could not see the rainbow
but I can still feel its happiness.

I awakened you, Boy,
during the night, remember,
just before the foal was born.

And you said to me,
"Come, Boy,
Circles is ready to foal.
The colt will be yours."

It was a long night of cold rain . . .

. . . and we put a blanket
over Circles, Grandfather,
to keep her warm.

Yes, Boy.
As the sun
came through the clouds,
the foal was born . . .

. . . and a rainbow
danced across the sky.

It was a good sign, Boy.

And I named the little wet foal . . .
Rainbow!

You have trained her well, Boy.

Rainbow is smart, Grandfather.

Like you.
She is good at remembering.

Rainbow is my eyes, Grandfather.
She takes me to the sheep,
wherever they are,
and when I am ready,
she finds the way home.

No one thought you could teach her
to race, Boy . . .

. . . but I did, Grandfather!
Every day, day after day,
we followed you along the trail . . .
And you let me hold the reins.

You traced the trails
in your mind, Boy,
both you and Rainbow.

Yes, Grandfather,
we learned the trails by heart . . .
up South Mountain to Granite Rock . . .
down the steep shortcut
to Meadow-of-Blue-Flowers . . .
then straight across the Red Flats
to Lightning-Split-Tree . . .
then down the Switchbacks
to the canyon trail . . .
and on around to the finish line.
I learned from Rainbow when to turn
by the pull of her neck
and by counting her gallops.
Now tell me again about the race,
Grandfather.

It was a tribal day, Boy.
You and the other boys
were at the starting line . . .
but you pulled back.

I was afraid, Grandfather,
until you called to me.
Tell me again what you said.

      I said,
       "Don't be afraid, Boy!
        Trust your darkness!
        Go like the wind!"

And I leaned forward
on Rainbow's neck.
I grabbed her mane tight,
and I said, "Go, Rainbow, go!"
I could feel the
pushing and crowding
and galloping thunder
all around me.
Rainbow and I
went twisting, turning,
galloping, galloping, galloping,
counting the gallops . . .
remembering the way . . .
And what did the people say, Grandfather?

      They said,
       "Who is that boy riding bareback . . .
        racing the race with all of his heart?"

And you said,
"That is Boy-Strength-of-Blue-Horses . . .
He and his horse are together like one."

      Yes, Boy, that is what I said.

But I didn't win, Grandfather.

      No, but you rode like the wind.

The wind is my friend, Grandfather.
It throws back my hair
and laughs in my face.

      You see the wind better than I, Boy.

I finished the race, hot and dusty,
sweat dripping from my face . . .

      And you were smiling, Boy!

I wasn't afraid, Grandfather.
I could see through the dark
every turn of the race.
Rainbow and I knew the way.

      You were crossing dark mountains, Boy!

Tell me again what you told me then.
I like to hear it over and over.

      I said,
      "Boy-Strength-of-Blue-Horses,
      you have raced darkness and won!
      You now can see with your heart,
      feel a part of all that surrounds you.
      Your courage lights the way."

And what did the grandmothers say?

      You tell me, Boy.
      I know you remember.

Yes, I remember, Grandfather.
They said,
"This boy walks in beauty.
His dreams are more beautiful
than rainbows and sunsets."

Now, Boy . . .
now that the story has been told again,
I will tie another knot
in the counting rope.
When the rope is filled with knots,
you will know the story by heart
and can tell it to yourself.

So that I will grow stronger, Grandfather?

Yes . . . stronger . . . strong enough
to cross the dark mountains.

I always feel strong
when you are with me, Grandfather.

I will not always be with you, Boy.

No, Grandfather,
don't ever leave me.
What will I do without you?

You will never be alone, Boy.
My love, like the strength of blue horses,
will always surround you.

ISBN 0-590-99448-4

Text copyright © 1966 and 1987 by Bill Martin Jr. and John Archambault.
Illustrations copyright © 1987 by Ted Rand.
All rights reserved. Published by Scholastic Inc., 555 Broadway, New York, NY 10012, by arrangement with Henry Holt and Company, Inc.
SCHOLASTIC and associated logos are trademarks and/or registe trademarks of Scholastic Inc.

A different version of *Knots On a Counting Rope* was first published in 1966.

12 11 10 9 8   0 1/0

Printed in the U.S.A.

Designer: Marc Cheshire